BERNIE
the flying Squirrel

By Bill Lynam

Illustrations by Russ Miller

ACKNOWLEDGEMENTS:

Hats off to Tom Fox, Darlis Sailors, Dawn Perlak, Elaine Jordan, Maria Lynam and Jennifer Longworth for their many contributions.

First Edition

Library of Congress Control Number: 2018930649

ISBN 978-0-9912574-1-6

Printed in the United States of America

PUYUP PUBLISHING COMPANY
4875 Comanche Trail
Prescott, AZ 86301
www.bill-lynam.com

For Kyle Evan Lynam, Jr.

IT WAS A BRIGHT, SUNNY DAY and the leaves on the trees were turning to yellow and gold. The leaves moved in the wind. A few let loose and floated to the ground. A colorful carpet was beginning to form on the forest floor.

All the animals in the woods were busy gathering food for the winter, including Bernie, the flying squirrel. But it was difficult for Bernie since he had a problem.

Two weeks before, while flying from tree limb to tree limb, Bernie saw a squirrel flying in the opposite direction carrying a **monster** acorn.

Bernie, not watching where he was flying, but staring at the acorn instead, hit a big oak tree and crashed, fall
i
n
g
to the ground.

Other squirrels on the ground gathering nuts saw Bernie crash land and called for an ambulance.

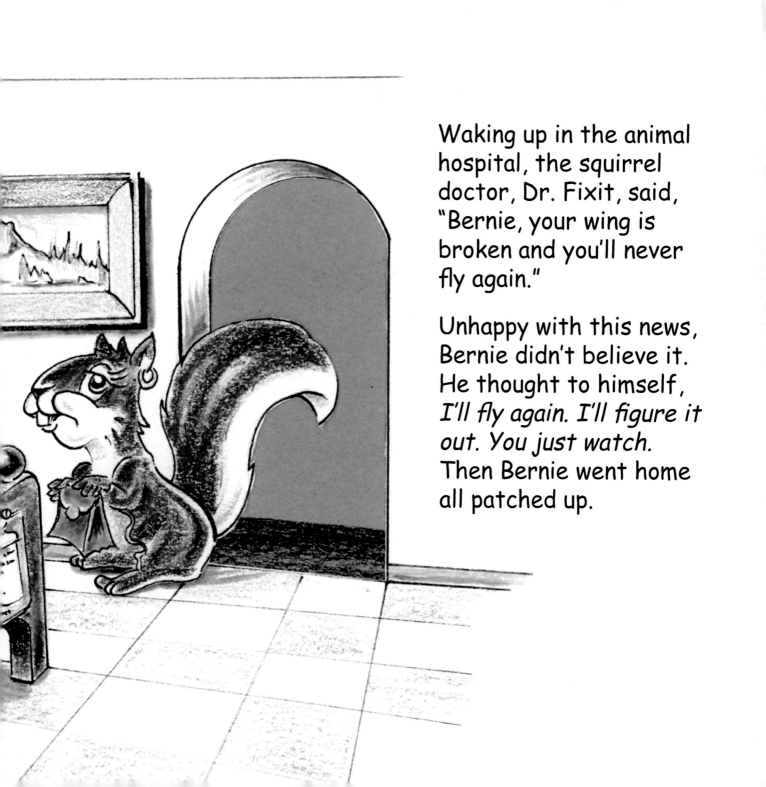

Waking up in the animal hospital, the squirrel doctor, Dr. Fixit, said, "Bernie, your wing is broken and you'll never fly again."

Unhappy with this news, Bernie didn't believe it. He thought to himself, *I'll fly again. I'll figure it out. You just watch.* Then Bernie went home all patched up.

Bernie still had to gather acorns for the winter. He ran around the ground under the oak trees looking for his favorite food. But all the other squirrels had gathered up most of the nuts and he couldn't find enough to take back to his tree home for the winter. Bernie almost cried until he spotted a sign tacked to a tree.

Bernie hunted until he found six acorns. Not enough for the winter, but enough to enter the contest, plus one for a snack. He didn't lose any time and hurried as fast as he could over to the big white oak to enter. There he found a long line. It was the only day to enter and it was almost closing time. Hundreds of squirrels had signed up.

Bernie's friend, Julie, was at the
head of the line and saw he was hurt.
She ran over to him, "Hurry Bernie, they're
going to close the entry booth any minute now."

She brought him up to the booth and told the squirrel in charge, "My friend Bernie is hurt. If he has to wait in line, he won't be able to enter the contest. So, please take him instead of me," she begged.

"OK," said the squirrel in charge, "Five acorns, please."

Bernie emptied his pouch and put four acorns on the counter. He'd gotten so hungry looking for acorns, he'd eaten two of the six he'd found for snacks.

"Sorry, Bernie. That's not enough. The entry fee is five acorns. Next contestant," the squirrel in charge said.

"Hold it, Mr. Squirrel," Julie said, and gave him one of her acorns to make it all five acorns needed for the entry fee.

"Here is your ticket, Bernie. Be on the starting line tree branch next Monday at 8:00 A.M." With that, the squirrel in charge shut the entry booth and put up a sign that said: CLOSED.

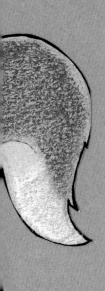

Bernie still had a problem. How was he going to fly with a busted wing? When he got home, he told his mother about the contest.

"You are going to win this contest. I'll make you a fine jacket. When you jump off the tree, the sleeve will turn into a wing and you'll fly better than all of them."

His mother went to her sewing machine and soon had a jacket with a wing sleeve ready for Bernie. He put it on. It fit just right. "Thank you, Mama," Bernie said.

"Wheee," he yelled, as he jumped off the high branch and flew in circles, landing softly on the ground. "Boy, am I ready for the contest now," he shouted up to his mother watching from her tree house.

On Monday, all the contestants were at the starting line. The big oak tree's branches sagged from all the squirrels perched next to each other, fidgeting, ready to fly. Bernie arrived just in time and ran up the tree to join them. They were all waiting for the judge to say: "GO!" The squirrels were ready to jump, to see who could fly the farthest.

Below, on the forest floor, the contest workers were waiting at different distances from the big tree. They would mark where each flying squirrel landed.

The contestants were nervous and anxious because each squirrel wanted to win the prize. They were trembling on the branches, ready to fly. One of the squirrels was so nervous, he started flying before the official start.

The judge bellowed at the too eager squirrel, "Mr., you are disqualified. You flew too soon. Go home." The early flyer flew away, crying.

Finally, the judge said, "Get ready, get set, go!" And all the flying squirrels jumped into the air, all except Bernie. He waited just a second longer, then he jumped too.

He flew behind all of them in his new jacket.
His sleeve extended, floating on the wake of
air his fellow squirrels left behind them.

One by one, the contestants lost lift and floated down, and landed short. The workers on the ground marked their landing place. But Bernie flew on, held aloft by the cushion of disturbed air from the other flyers. He kept flying, helped by his magic wing, until there was just the leader and himself. When the lead squirrel lost his lift, he landed. But Bernie kept going and almost overflew the forest. He let himself set down at the finish line where the prize bag of acorns rested.

All the animals in the forest hooted and cried and clapped for Bernie, Julie most of all. She gave him a big hug. He'd won.

Bernie knew now he would never be troubled
by some setback, since there is always another
way to find a solution. He also knew what he had
to do. He would share his prize with his friend
Julie and his mother, who made it all possible.

Suggested Questions for Parents, Teachers, and Others to Discuss with the Reader

These are some questions you can ask your child or student about their reading. Ask a few to engage in conversation to get feedback on understanding and comprehension skills.

Only use the questions you wish or that you think are appropriate.

Questions to Ask Before Reading:

- Based on the title and Bernie's picture on the cover, what do you think will happen in the book?
- Why do you think that?
- Who else do you think will be in the book?
- Do you think there will be a problem in the story? Why?
- Do you already know something about the book?
- Could what happens in the story, happen in your family? How?

Questions to Ask During Reading:

- What is going on in the story? Can you tell me?
- What do you think will happen next in the story?
- How do you think the story will end?
- What do you think Bernie did?
- If you were Bernie, what would you have done?
- What questions do you have about the story?
- Did the story go the way you thought it would? Why or why not?
- How do you think the story will go?

QUESTIONS TO ASK AFTER READING:

- Do you like the title for the book? If you would change the title, what would it be?
- Were your guesses about the book correct? Which guesses were right and which did you have to change?
- Was there a problem and did it get solved?
- How was the problem solved or not?
- What happened because of the problem?
- Did any of the characters change through the story?
- Who changed and how did they change?
- What is the most important point that the author is trying to make in this story?
- What was your favorite part? Why?
- If you could change one part of the story, what would you change?
- Can you tell the story in sequential order? That is, what happened first, then next and so on.
- Is there a character in the story that reminds you of someone you know?
- If so, who are they, and why do you think that?
- Did the pictures in this book help you understand the story?

MORE WAYS TO INTERACT AND DEMONSTRATE UNDERSTANDING:

- Draw a picture of a favorite scene from the story.
- Write a follow-up story.
- Write a review of the book.
- Write a letter or postcard to the author.
- Act out a memorable part of the book.

BIOS

BILL LYNAM, a writer and teacher, taught adult education in upstate New York. He is the author of central Arizona histories for a local newspaper and numerous magazine articles. His Steampunk Mashup, a collection of science fiction short stories was published in 2017 on Amazon and Kindle. He co-authored Footloose Pilgrims, a coming of age travelogue published in 2014 also on Amazon and Kindle. Bill and his wife, Maria, live in Prescott, AZ.

RUSS MILLER, a syndicated columnist and writer, worked for Disney and Marvel Comics. He is the originator of Oddly Enough, an illustrated column of phenomenal events. Lately, he has been seen in a kilt playing bagpipes. A motorcycle enthusiast, he often is surrounded by a menagerie of pets and livestock. He and his wife, Renee, live in Chino Valley, AZ.

Made in the USA
Lexington, KY
30 August 2018